THANKS

Wonderful **Whiting**

First U.S. edition 2014

Library of Congress Catalog Card Number 2013944022
ISBN 978-0-7636-6781-8

CCP 19 18 17 16 15 14
10 9 8 7 6 5 4 3 2 1

Printed in Shenzhen, Guangdong, China

This book was typeset in Caslon Antique.
The illustrations were done in pencil, ink, and collage.

Candlewick Press
99 Dover Street
Somerville, Massachusetts 02144

visit us at www.candlewick.com

EELES

Nutritious
&
Delicious

FOR YOU

A PERFECT PLACE FOR TED

LEILA RUDGE

Candlewick Press

Ted had been at the pet store for as long as he could remember.

He was a smart dog with his own sweater,

and he did his best to make a good impression.

But there were so many other dogs that **nobody noticed** Ted.

This is not where I belong, thought Ted.

So he decided to find somewhere perfect.

The following morning, Ted joined the **circus.**

The big top was magnificent.

The audience cheered as the circus dogs
flew through the air.
But **nobody noticed** Ted
on his popcorn box.

So Ted entered a **pet pageant** instead.

After the bubbles

and the blow-dry,

Ted looked sensational.

But the judges preferred the
poodles with pom-poms.
And **nobody** took any photos of Ted.

So Ted got a job as a **guard dog.**

He kept an eye out for strangers.

And checked the newspaper for anything suspicious.

But even the burglar **didn't notice** Ted.

I don't belong anywhere, thought Ted.

So he stopped searching for somewhere perfect
and headed back toward the pet store.

But just then,
something caught Ted's eye. . . .

WANTED

FURRY FRIEND
FOR DOT

**FURRY FRIEND
FOR DOT**

Must enjoy
long walks and
ball games.

♥ ♥ ♥

Ted did his best to make a good impression.
And Dot **noticed.**

They **hung out** all afternoon.

And became **fabulous friends.**

As Ted arrived at his new home, he couldn't believe his luck.
This is where I belong, thought Ted.

He had finally found somewhere . . .

puuuurrrrrfect.